W9-BZC-042

THIS CANDLEWICK BOOK BELONGS TO:

_____

_____

_____

To Teacher Joan, who loves pets
D. D.

In memory of my beloved friend Trina
M. H.

Text copyright © 2006 by Dayle Ann Dodds
Illustrations copyright © 2006 by Marylin Hafner

First paperback edition 2010

The Library of Congress has cataloged the hardcover edition as follows:

Dodds, Dayle Ann.
Teacher's pets / Dayle Ann Dodds ; illustrated by Marylin Hafner. —1st ed.
p. cm.
Summary: A teacher invites her students to bring their pets in each Monday for sharing day,
but by the end of the year, she has a classroom full of "forgotten" animals.
ISBN 978-0-7636-2252-7 (hardcover)
[1. Pets—Fiction. 2. Schools—Fiction.] I. Hafner, Marylin, ill. II. Title.
PZ7.D66285 Too 2006
[E]—dc22   2005053186

ISBN 978-0-7636-4631-8 (paperback)

09 10 11 12 13 14 CCP 10 9 8 7 6 5 4 3 2 1

Printed in Shenzhen, Guangdong, China

This book was typeset in Clichee.
The illustrations were done in ink, watercolor, and colored pencil.

Candlewick Press
99 Dover Street
Somerville, Massachusetts 02144

visit us at www.candlewick.com

Teacher's Pets

Dayle Ann Dodds

illustrated by Marylin Hafner

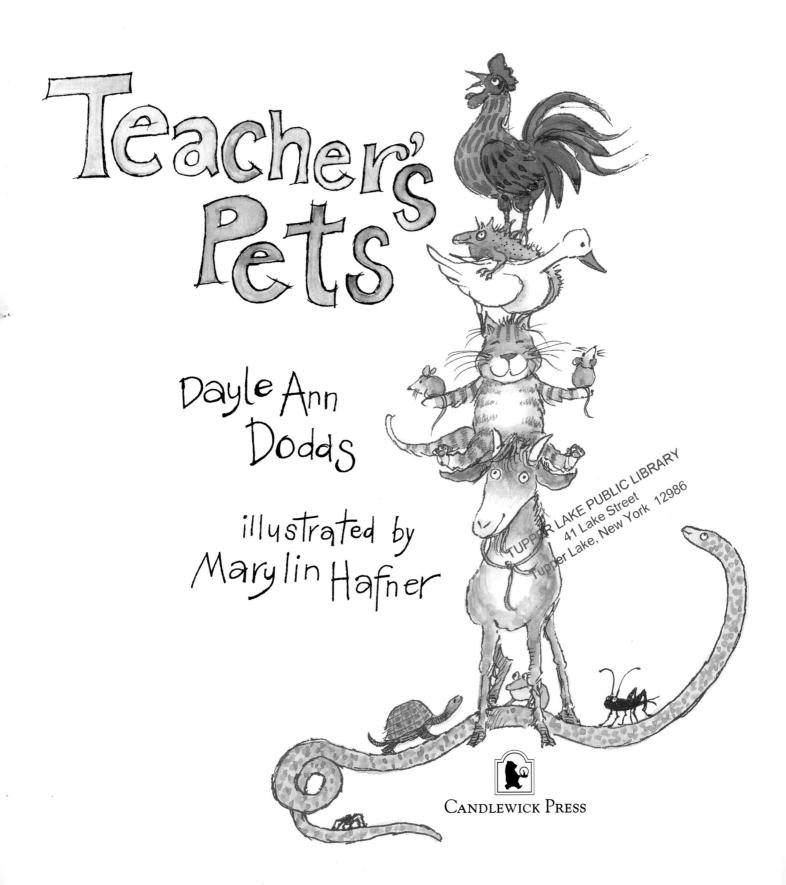

CANDLEWICK PRESS

Monday was sharing day in Miss Fry's class.
"You may bring something special," said Miss Fry.

"May we share a pet?" Winston asked.

"Yes," said Miss Fry. "But just for the day."

On Monday, Winston brought in his pet rooster.
"I call him Red. He eats corn, and he crows.
The neighbors say he crows too much."

"What a wonderful pet," said Miss Fry.
"We're happy he can visit us today."

But that afternoon, after all the children had left,
there was Red, still sitting on his roost near
Miss Fry's desk.

She sprinkled corn in Red's dish,
then locked the door and went home
to her quiet little house.

On Tuesday, Winston told Miss Fry, "The neighbors wonder if Red can stay at school for a while."

"Of course," said Miss Fry. "How lucky for us."

The next Monday was Patrick's turn. "My tarantula's name is Vincent. He likes to eat bugs and hide inside my mother's slippers."

"What a wonderful pet," said Miss Fry. "Don't forget to take Vincent home with you at the end of the day."

But that afternoon, after all the children had left, there was Vincent, still sitting in his jar on Miss Fry's desk.

She gave Vincent a big juicy bug, sprinkled corn in Red's dish, then locked the door and went home to her quiet little house.

On Tuesday, Patrick told Miss Fry, "My mother says Vincent likes her slippers too much. We're wondering if he can stay at school for a few days."

"Of course," said Miss Fry. "How lucky for us."

The next week, Roger brought in his cricket.

"His name is Moe," said Roger. "He eats leaves from the garden and sings *chirrup-chirrup* all night long."

"What a wonderful pet," said Miss Fry.

That afternoon, after all the children had left,
Miss Fry noticed Moe sitting in his box on the table.

Miss Fry looked at Moe. He almost seemed to smile.
"Welcome to our class, Moe."

Right before her eyes,
he did a huge somersault—
up, up in the air.

"Bravo!" said Miss Fry.

She gave fresh green leaves to Moe
and a big juicy bug to Vincent, sprinkled
corn in Red's dish, then locked the door
and went home to her quiet little house.

The next day, Roger said to Miss Fry, "My mother says Moe chirps too much."

"He's welcome to visit as long as he likes," said Miss Fry.

And so it went.

Alia shared her pet goat named Gladys. It said *Baaaaaa!* and ate her sister's homework.

Amanda shared her pet dachshund. It liked to chew bones and the pillows on her aunt Judy's new sofa.

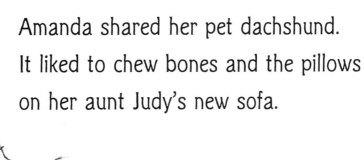

Jerry brought in his pet boa constrictor. It never made a sound. No one knew exactly what it liked to eat, but Jerry said his father's expensive tropical fish had suddenly disappeared one day.

There was Megan's cat,

Mitchell's mice,

Daniel's ducks,

and Tom's iguana.

Lily's monkey,

Frankie's frog,

Terrence's turtle . . .

and something square and fuzzy that Avery
brought in.

"It looks like a kitchen sponge," said Bruce.
"A *really old* kitchen sponge."

"It's my pet," said Avery, and that was that.

Before long, Miss Fry's classroom was bursting with the happy noises of all the children's pets.

On Parents' Night, the mothers and fathers walked around the classroom with great big smiles on their faces.

"Isn't it great," they said, "that Miss Fry loves pets so?"

chirrup

Only Roger's cricket sat quietly in his box. "You must miss your garden," Miss Fry said.

Chirrup, Moe said softly. He crawled under one of his shiny green leaves.

On the last day of school,
Miss Fry's class had a party
with balloons, hats, and
ice-cream cups.

"Goodbye, children!" Miss Fry sang out.
"Have a nice summer . . . *and don't forget to*

take
home
your
Pets!

I sure won't.

One by one, the children disappeared, and with them went their pets.

"No more pets," said Miss Fry. She looked around the quiet, empty room.

Then Miss Fry noticed a box sitting on her desk.

She peeked inside. A little face
looked up at her. It almost seemed
to smile.

A note inside read:

DEAR MISS FRY,
PLEASE TAKE
CARE
OF MOE.
HE LIKES YOU
BEST.

ROGER

"How lucky for me," said Miss Fry.

Moe did a huge somersault—up, up in the air.

Miss Fry carried her new pet to her quiet little house and placed him in the garden, among the rainbow of roses.

That night, Miss Fry opened her window.
She climbed into bed.
She turned off the lamp.

By the light of the moon,
from outside in the garden,
came a happy noise.

Chirrup-chirrup!

Dayle Ann Dodds is a former schoolteacher and holds a degree in early childhood development. She is the author of numerous picture books for children, including *Minnie's Diner: A Multiplying Menu*, *The Shape of Things*, and *The Great Divide: A Mathematical Marathon*. A friend who is a kindergarten teacher inspired her to write *Teacher's Pets*. As she explains, "The children in my friend's class kept bringing in pets to share and then leaving them in her care instead of taking them home. She hasn't had a visit from a tarantula or a boa constrictor yet, but you never know!" Dayle Ann Dodds lives in California.

Marylin Hafner grew up in a household of artists and musicians, and studied at the Pratt Institute. She is the creator of the Molly and Emmett characters featured in *Ladybug* magazine and the illustrator of more than one hundred books for children, including *Lunch Bunnies*, *Show and Tell Bunnies*, and *Tumble Bunnies*, all written by Kathryn Lasky. Marylin Hafner lives in Massachusetts.